Ten in the Den

For Joshua James
J. B.

Published by
PEACHTREE PUBLISHERS
1700 Chattahoochee Avenue
Atlanta, Georgia 30318-2112
www.peachtree-online.com

ISBN 1-56145-344-7

First published in Great Britain in 2005 by Orchard Books.

Printed in Singapore
10 9 8 7 6 5 4 3 2 1
First Edition

www.johnbutlerart.com

Library of Congress Cataloging-in-Publication Data

Butler, John, 1952-
Ten in the den / written and illustrated by John Butler.-- 1st ed.
p. cm.
Summary: One by one nine forest creatures fall out of bed when Little Mouse says "Roll over!"
ISBN 1-56145-344-7
1. Nursery rhymes. 2. Children's poetry. [1. Animals--Poetry. 2. Counting. 3. Nursery rhymes.] I. Title.
PZ8.3.B9788 Te2005
[E]--dc22
2004026868

Ten in the Den

John Butler

PEACHTREE
ATLANTA

There were **ten** in the den,
and the little mouse said,

"Roll over! Roll over!"
So they all rolled over and . . .

Rabbit fell out.

Floppetty,

hoppetty,

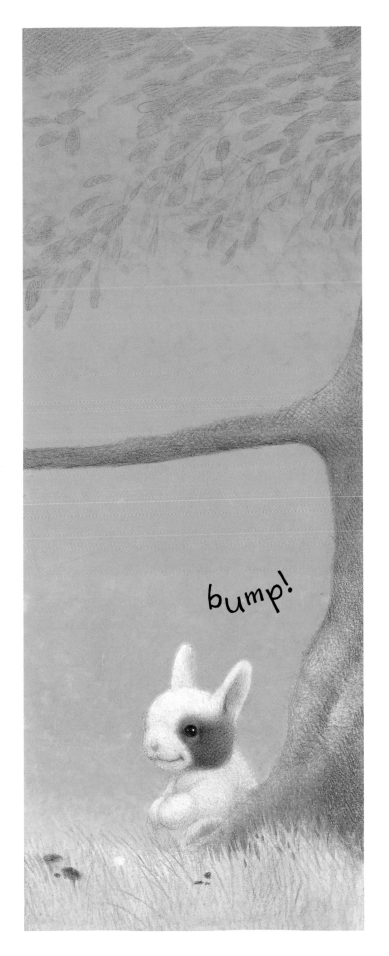

bump!

There were **nine** in the den,
and the little mouse said,

"Roll over! Roll over!"
So they all rolled over and . . .

Mole fell out.

Roly,

poly,

bump!

There were **eight** in the den,
and the little mouse said,

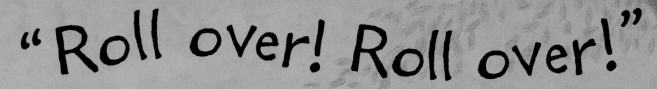

"Roll over! Roll over!"
So they all rolled over
and Beaver fell out.

Slippy, slidey, bump!

There were **seven** in the den,
and the little mouse said,

"Roll over!
Roll over!"

So they all rolled over and . . .

Badger fell out.

Bouncy,

pouncy,

bump!

There were **six** in the den,
and the little mouse said,

"Roll over! Roll over!"
So they all rolled over and . . .

Porcupine fell out.

Prickly,

tickly,

bump!

There were **five** in the den,
and the little mouse said,

"Roll over! Roll over!"
So they all rolled over and . . .

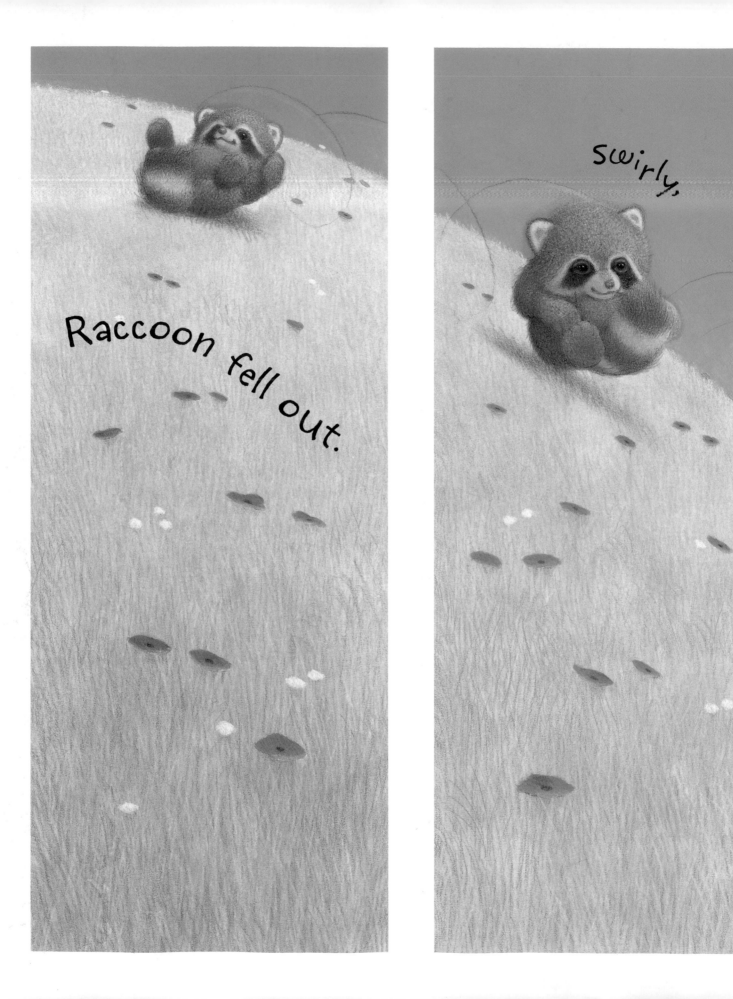

There were **four** in the den,
and the little mouse said,

"Roll over! Roll over!"
So they all rolled over and . . .

Fox fell out.

Rumbly,

tumbly,

bump!

There were **three** in the den,
and the little mouse said,

"Roll over! Roll over!"

So they all rolled over
and Squirrel fell out.

squiggly,

wiggly,

bump!

Bear fell out. Bumpety, thumpety,

There were **two** in the den,
and the little mouse said,

"Roll over!
Roll over!"

So they both rolled over and . . .

bump!

There was **one** in the den,
and the little mouse sniffed,

"I miss my friends!"

So he rolled over and scampered out.

"Wait

for

me!"

There were **ten** friends again,
and the little mouse yawned . . .

"Night night.
Sleep tight!"

So they all snuggled together and . . .

fell fast asleep.
ZZZZzzzzzzzzzzzz

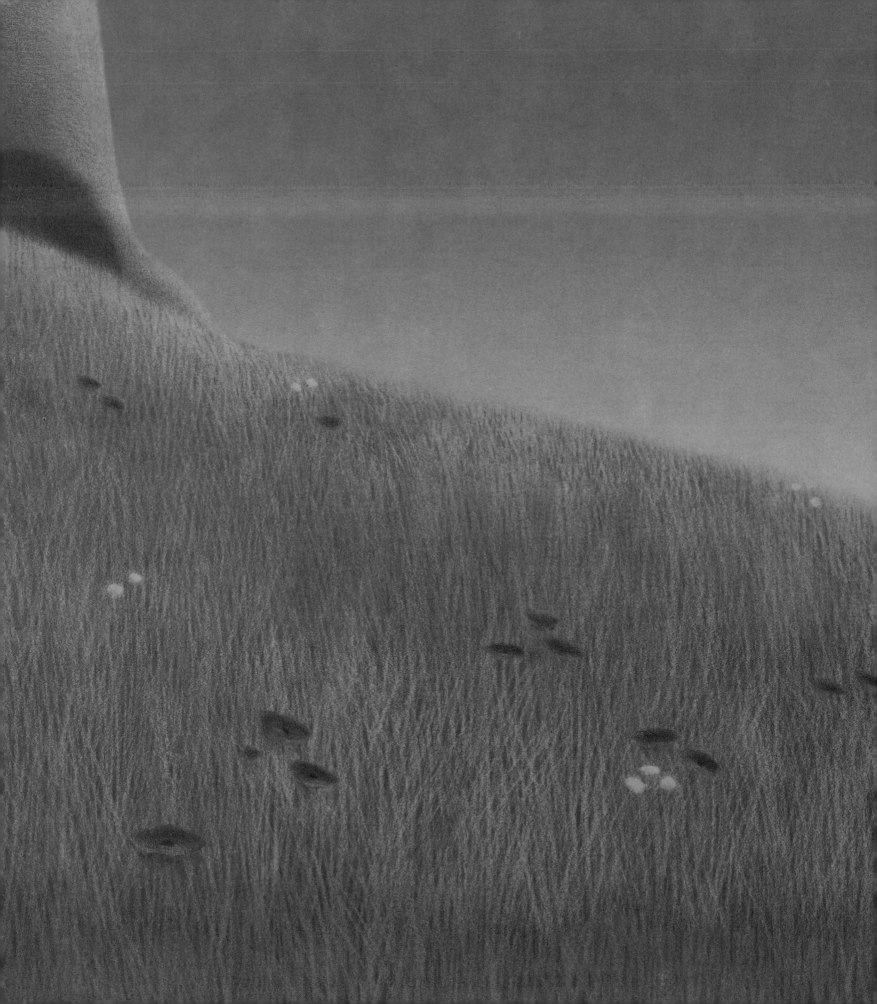